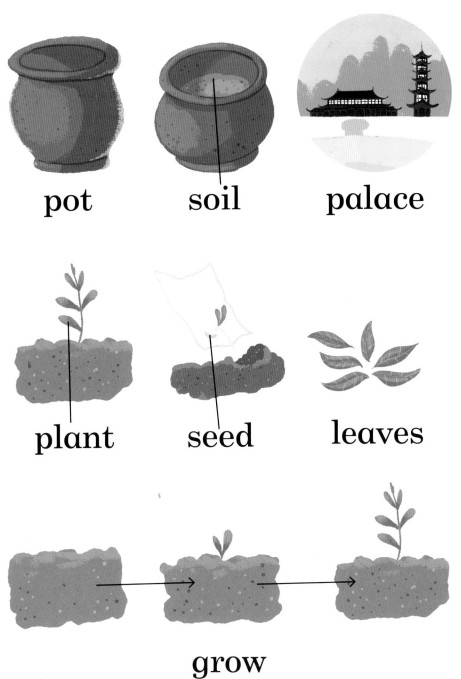

pot

soil

palace

plant

seed

leaves

grow

The emperor is in
his garden.
"I'm old," he says. "I have
no child."

Ladybird  Readers

The Empty Pot

Picture words

the emperor

Jun

Jun's mother

Jun's father

carry

empty

4

"How do I find a
new emperor?"

"Boys!" the emperor writes. "I'm choosing the new emperor. Come to my palace and get a seed, please."

11

12

"A seed?" says Jun.

"Yes," his mother says. "You grow beautiful plants, Jun. Go to the palace."

Jun walks to the palace with many boys.

"I want a seed," say the boys.
"I can be the new emperor."

"Have a seed," says
the emperor.

"Go home. Put it in a pot.
Come back with your pot
after one year."

Jun puts his seed in his favorite pot.

Jun watches his pot.

The boys have leaves in their pots. But they are not from the emperor's seeds . . .

Jun watches his pot.

"That's good soil and water,
Father," he says.

"Look, no leaves," says Jun.

"Don't worry," says
his father.

After one year, the boys carry
their pots to the palace.
Jun goes with his empty pot.

"I like this empty pot," says
the emperor.

"Why?" people ask.

"Well," says the emperor.
"My seeds are old and bad.
You CAN'T grow them."

"Well done, Jun! You're a good boy—and you are the new emperor!" says the happy old emperor.

Activities

The key below describes the skills practiced in each activity.

Spelling and writing

Reading

Speaking

Critical thinking

Preparation for the Cambridge Young Learners exams

1 **Read the sentences and match them with the correct person. Write 1—4.** 📖

1 He is the emperor.

2 He is Jun.

3 She is Jun's mother.

4 He is Jun's father.

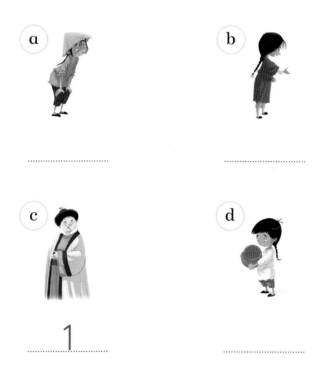

a

....

b

....

c

1
....

d

....

2 Put a ✓ by the things in the garden. 📖

1	flower	✓	**2**	car	☐
3	horses	☐	**4**	leaves	☐
5	plant	☐	**6**	pot	☐
7	sea	☐	**8**	seed	☐
9	soil	☐	**10**	street	☐
11	train	☐	**12**	tree	☐
13	TV	☐	**14**	water	☐

3 **Circle the correct sentences.**

1  **a** The pot is empty.

b The pot is not empty.

2  **a** This is a plant.

b This is not a plant.

3  **a** This is the emperor's palace.

b This is the emperor's pot.

4  **a** This is a flower.

b This is a seed.

4 **Look and read. Put a ☑ or a ☒ in the boxes.** 📖 🔖

1 He is carrying his pot. ☑

2 The emperor is in his palace. ☐

3 The plant is growing. ☐

4 The emperor is Jun's father. ☐

5 Jun lives here. ☐

5 **Look and read. Choose the correct words, and write them on the lines.** 📖 ✏️ ⬡

Jun walks to the palace with many boys.

"I want a seed," say the boys. "I can be the new emperor."

Jun   emperor   boys   seed

1 _____Jun_____ walks to the palace with many _____.

2 "I want a _____," say the boys. "I can be the new _____."

6 **Circle the correct pictures.**

1 He lives in a palace.

2 These grow on plants.

 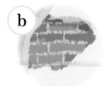 

3 You can grow a plant in it.

4 This helps plants grow.

  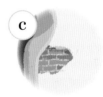

7 Write the missing letters.

r r   a v   e e   l a   p t

1  c a ..r.. ..r.. y

2  e m .... y

3  l e .... e s

4  p a .... c e

5  s .... d

8 Who says this?

the emperor | Jun | Jun's father | Jun's mother

1 "How do I find a new emperor?"

says _the emperor_.

2 "You grow beautiful plants,

Jun. Go to the palace,"

says _____.

3 "That's good soil and water, Father,"

says _____.

4 "Don't worry,"

says _____.

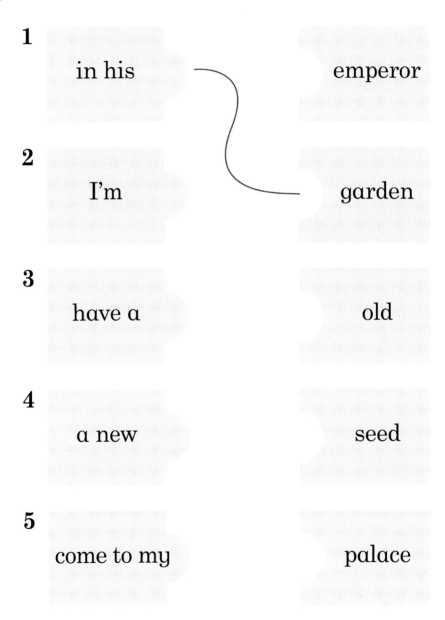

9 **Match the words.**

1 in his   emperor

2 I'm   garden

3 have a   old

4 a new   seed

5 come to my   palace

10 **Read the questions.**
Write the answers. 📖 ✏️ ✳️

"Boys!" the emperor writes. "I'm choosing the new emperor. Come to my palace and get a seed, please."

"A seed?" says Jun.

"Yes," his mother says. "You grow beautiful plants, Jun. Go to the palace."

1 Who does the emperor write to?

He writes to the boys.

2 Why does he write to them?

....

3 What can the boys get at the palace?

....

4 Who goes to the palace?

....

11 Write the correct sentences.

1 (choosing) (emperor) (I'm)

(new) (the) (.)

I'm choosing the new
emperor.

2 (to) (palace) (my) (Come) (.)

....

3 (beautiful) (grows) (Jun) (plants) (.)

....

4 (the) (to) (palace) (Go) (.)

....

5 (walks) (the) (to) (palace) (Jun) (.)

....

12 Look and read. Write *a* or *the*.

1 Jun walks to .... the .... palace with many boys.

2 "I want .... seed," say .... boys. "I can be .... new emperor."

3 "Have .... seed," says .... emperor.

4 "Go home. Put it in .... pot. Come back with your pot after one year."

13 Read the text. Choose the correct words and write them next to 1—5.

> puts   is   says   have   watches

Jun [1] .... puts .... his seed in his favorite pot. Jun [2] .... his pot. The boys [3] .... leaves in their pots. But they are not from the emperor's seeds . . . Jun watches his pot.

"That [4] .... good soil and water, Father," he [5] ....

14 **Circle the correct words.**

1 Jun says,

   a "Look, no leaves."

   b "Look, some leaves."

2 His father says,

   a "Don't worry."

   b "Oh, no."

3 The emperor says,

   a "I don't like this empty pot."

   b "I like this empty pot."

4 The emperor says,

   a "Well done, Jun! You're a bad boy."

   b "Well done, Jun! You're a good boy."

15 **Write _beautiful_, _good_, _happy_, _new_, or _old_.** 📖 ✏️

1 "I'm _____old_____," he says. "I have no child."

2 "How do I find a _____ emperor?"

3 "You grow _____ plants, Jun. Go to the palace."

4 "That's _____ soil and water, Father," he says.

5 The old emperor is _____ now.

16 **Order the story. Write 1—4.** 📖

.... He gives the boys some seeds.

.... Jun is the new emperor.

.... Jun's seed does not grow.

......1...... The old emperor wants a
new emperor.

17 Talk about the two pictures with a friend. How are they different? Use the words in the box. 🗨

old   young   boy   emperor
garden   house   big   small

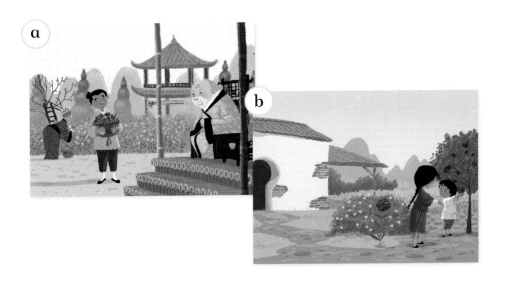

In picture a, there is an old man. In picture b, there is a young boy.

18 **Ask and answer the questions with a friend.**

1

What color is your home?

It is white.

2 Is it big or small?

3 Have you got a garden?

4 Are there plants in the garden?

19 Look and read. Write *yes* or *no*.

"Why?" people ask.

"Well," says the emperor. "My seeds are old and bad. You CAN'T grow them."

"Well done, Jun! You're a good boy—and you are the new emperor!" says the happy old emperor.

27

1 The emperor likes Jun's empty pot. .....yes....

2 The seeds are new and good. ....

3 You can grow them. ....

4 Jun is the new emperor. ....

5 The old emperor is happy. ....

Ladybird Readers

Visit www.ladybirdeducation.co.uk
for more FREE Ladybird Readers resources

✓ Digital edition of every title*

✓ Audio tracks (US/UK)

✓ Answer keys

✓ Lesson plans

✓ Role-plays

✓ Classroom display material

✓ Flashcards

✓ User guides

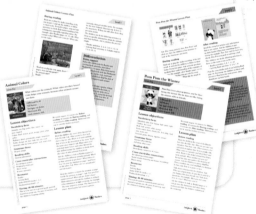

Register and sign up to the newsletter to receive your FREE classroom resource pack!

*Ladybird Readers series only. Not applicable to *Peppa Pig* books.
Digital versions of Ladybird Readers books available once book has been purchased.